TULLY AND ME

WRITTEN AND ILLUSTRATED BY KEELEY SHAW

Copyright © 2019 by Keeley Shaw

All rights reserved. This book or any portion thereof
may not be reproduced or used in any manner whatsoever
without the express written permission of the publisher
except for the use of brief quotations in a book review.

ISBN: 9780578494159

First Printing, 2019

Keeleyshaw.com

For the joyful turtle connoisseur, the strong
and persistent fighter and all the special people who opened my heart
without a word.

My friend Tully is different from me but we live side by side near a pond and oak tree.

WHEN THE BIRDS SING THEIR SONGS
I SING ALONG TOO.
la la la

AND JUMP WITH THE FROGS
JUST NOT LIKE THEY DO.

TULLY LIKES WINDY DAYS MORE THAN ME.

BECAUSE THE WIND BLOWS THE PINWHEEL
THAT SPINS NEAR THE TREE.

HE WAVES HIS ARMS AROUND AND AROUND...

UNTIL HE GETS SO TIRED
HE FALLS TO THE GROUND.

One day I asked Tully to play hide and seek

BUT HE WAS COUNTING MARCHING ANTS
AND DIDN'T WANT TO SPEAK.

He was counting the ants again and again..
1 2 3 4 5 6 7 8 9 10!

SUDDENLY THE LAWN MOWER CAME ROARING BY
TO CUT THE GRASS THAT GREW TOO HIGH.

TULLY DID NOT LIKE THAT SOUND
SO HE STARTED TO SCREAM
TO CALM HIMSELF DOWN.

THAT DIDN'T WORK SO HE STARTED TO CRY...
HE NEEDED TO RUN, HE NEEDED TO HIDE.

SO HE DUCKED IN HIS SHELL
WHERE HE FELT SAFE INSIDE.

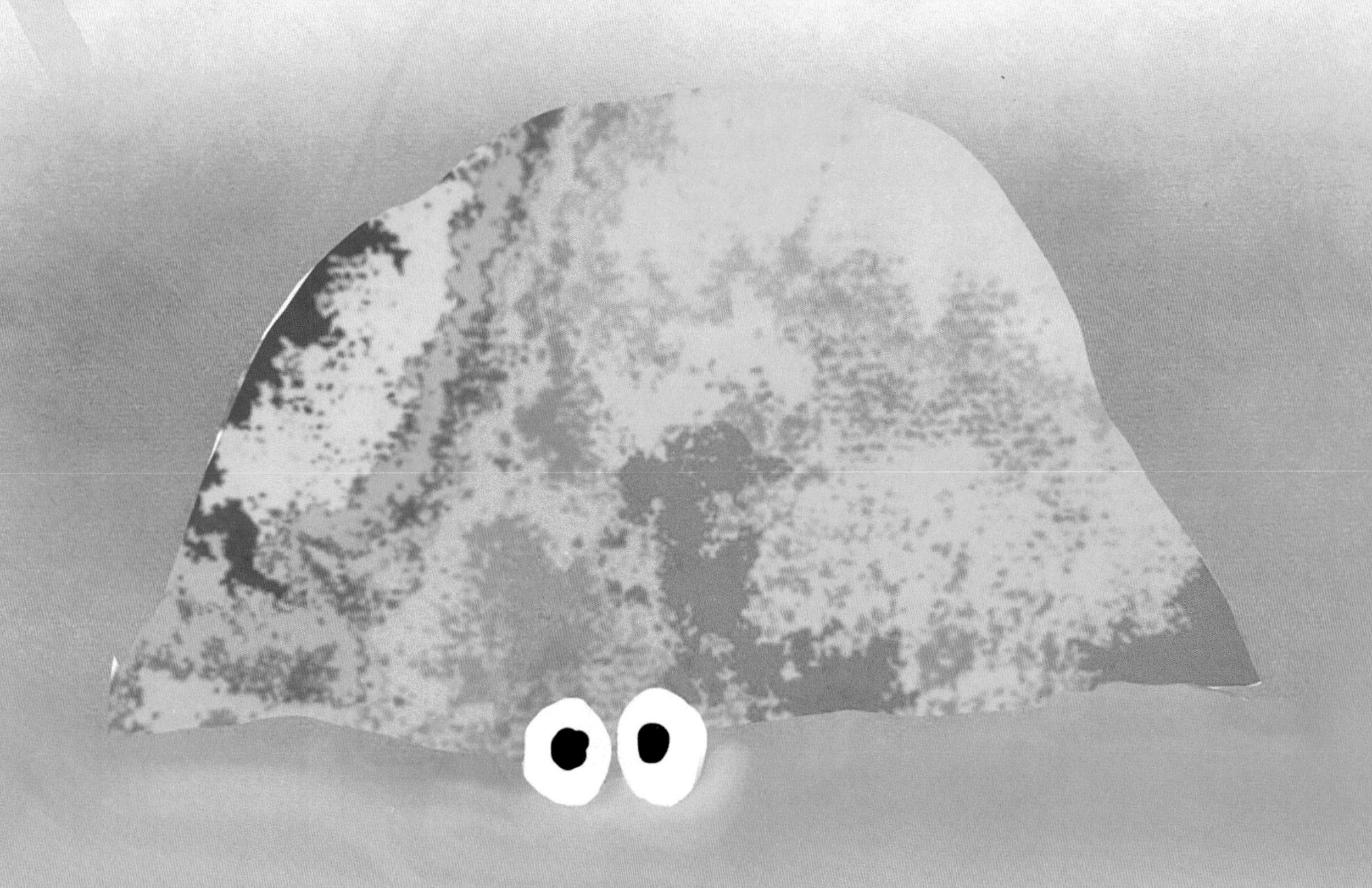

I thought and I thought, "What can I do!"
And the mower came closer and the loud sound grew!

I WALKED UP TO TULLY AND KNOCKED ON HIS SHELL.
AND SAID, "LET'S GO FOR A WALK DOWN OUR FAVORITE TRAIL."

THAT DIDN'T WORK, HE STAYED OUT OF SIGHT...

WHAT IF HE STAYS IN HIS SHELL ALL NIGHT?

TULLY LIKED COUNTING AGAIN AND AGAIN
SO I WILL COUNT...1 2 3 4 5 6 7 8 9 10.

TULLY LOVED COUNTING SO HE POKED HIS HEAD OUT

AND WHEN THE MOWER CAME BY, ONE TO TEN WE WOULD SHOUT!

JUST WATCH THE WHEELS, AROUND THEY GO.
JUST LIKE THE PINWHEEL...

THEY ROLL AND ROLL
AND ROLL...

AND THE WHEELS ON THE MOWER
WENT AROUND AND AROUND

UNTIL IT ROLLED AWAY
AND TOOK WITH IT THE SOUND.

THEN THE WIND BLEW AGAIN THROUGH THE LEAVES ON THE TREE
AND I SMILED AT TULLY AND HE SMILED BACK AT ME.

TULLY AND I ARE DIFFERENT,
THAT WE DON'T HIDE

BUT A SMILE FEELS THE SAME
ON THE INSIDE.

ABOUT THE AUTHOR

KEELEY SHAW IS AN ARTIST, ILLUSTRATOR, AND WRITER. SHE HOLDS A MASTER OF ARTS IN SPECIAL EDUCATION. SHE HAS HAD THE PRIVILEGE OF WORKING WITH INDIVIDUALS ON THE AUTISM SPECTRUM WHICH HEAVILY INFLUENCED THIS WORK.

CPSIA information can be obtained at www.ICGtesting.com
Printed in the USA
LVIW011947240220
648044LV00017B/807